The

Legend

of

Peter Mouse

Jeff Woodbridge

Front Cover by Nils Richter.
Email: nirryc@gmail.com

ISBN: 9798353797913

PublishNation
www.publishnation.co.uk

McQueen

The girl put away her pen and closed the book she had been writing in. She got down from her chair and put the book and the pen case into a satchel, ready for school the next day.

'Night, my lovely man', she said quietly as she picked up the cat off the back of the armchair her mum was softly snoring in.

She gently lowered the old cat onto his multi-cushioned bed under a radiator in the corner of the room, kissed the back of his head and turned to her dad.

'I've finished my homework and Queenie's in his basket, I'm off to bed.

Night dad' she said as she kissed the back of his head on her way past.

'Night honey, sleep well', he replied without taking his eyes off the TV.

She left the room, pulling the door so it was only just open and went to her bedroom.

McQueen sat up in his bed and started licking his fur. He wasn't going to be kept in tonight. He was going out and needed to be in good condition. He had a mission.

He coughed a furball onto the floor beside his basket, then urinated on it. No point in messing his bed when he can leave it for the humans to clear up tomorrow or whenever.

After all, he had lived here longer than anyone else in this school and he felt entitled to do as he pleased. When the girl and her family moved into the caretakers' quarters, they had agreed to look after the cat in his old age, and he was well aware of it too.

With his coat sorted, he stretched forward then back, making his muscles tense then relax ready for the evenings' entertainment.

Silently, he padded behind the chair where the human was watching other humans with a ball on a field.

He pushed open the door with his nose and out to where he could access the school.

At 16yrs old, he was no longer in his prime, although he would never admit to that. He had been in this school all his life.

His job had been referred to as a 'Mouser', and he had spent his entire life catching rodents, moths and birds that had managed to infiltrate the school, and he had loved his work.

Killing was his favourite pastime. He did it as often as he could, which wasn't as much these days, since the school had outlawed the method as 'old-fashioned', and now employed a human to do the work with bait and traps.

Apparently, it was no longer acceptable to leave bits of victims laid around the school for the children to find when they came in, in the mornings.

McQueen didn't care. He felt no sense of belonging to either the girl, her family, or the school. He had grown quite grumpy as the years had gone by, and only considered the humans as a feeding and resting station in between his hunting forays.

Tonight, he was going around the classrooms. He had heard noises behind the walls, particularly in classroom 6, where he could smell the scent of mice and some of them would be young, juicy, and tender.

He noiselessly padded down the corridor. On both sides, against the walls were the wooden lockers the children used to store their gym kits in. The classroom doors were open, ready for the cleaners to come in at 7 o'clock in the morning.

He slowed as he approached classroom 6 and peered carefully around the door.

There it was. He knew he was right. He could always trust his nose. There was a mouse scurrying around under the desks and chairs, eating an awful lot of mess that the children had left behind on the floor.

He quickly and quietly closed the distance between them. The mouse hadn't heard him. This was going to be an easy kill. He was really enjoying himself.

'Weel, hellooo, and what d'we 'ave 'ere noo?' his Scottish accent, loud in the quiet of the school, as he swung a paw with its' claws extended at the mouse.

Startled, the mouse jumped instinctively, turned in the air and ran.

McQueen had been surprised by that move. He'd expected his dinner to sit and die quietly.

Peter Mouse

Peter Mouse sat in his glass tank leaning against his running wheel, looking out of the window, and dreamed of being free. He really wanted to be outside where the grass grows long, and the plants grow wild.

His tank was really an old disused aquarium, 60cm x 30cm and 30cm high as well, that sat on a shelf at the back of classroom 6 of Woodside Road school. It was next to an empty wire bird cage that hadn't had an occupier for many years.

The tank had a wooden lid that didn't fit very well and a hole in the centre where a lamp had once been. It now allowed fresh air to circulate and that helped Peter to stay cool.

The bird cage was where he was put, while the children cleaned out his tank and put in new shavings for his bedding, and this was where he first saw himself in a mirror.

He found that if he took a run-up, he could jump up at the vertical bars of the cage, until his feet found the single horizontal wire, and he could push himself off that onto a wooden perch near the top. This is where the mirror was fixed, and at first when he looked, he thought there was another mouse in with him, and he turned around so quickly looking for it, he almost slipped off the perch.

But the main advantage of the cage was that from the wooden perch he could see all around the classroom, something he couldn't do from the floor of his tank. It meant he could see the children that were working on his home. He could see the teacher's desk and the chairs and desks where the children sat.

This gave Peter a perspective of the classroom he hadn't seen before, and he saved a mental picture of it to his memory.

One day a child had brought in a hamster wheel and put it in the centre of his tank for him to exercise on. Peter had been delighted.

Well, once he got used to it, he was, and he would run and run in the wheel for minutes at a time. It didn't take long for him to build up his strength and fitness. He was eating seeds and pieces of fruit and quite soon grew into a quick-witted mouse, full of energy and curiosity.

He had a ball to play with too. A white ping-pong ball with a dent in one side and one day a wooden pencil got dropped in and he really liked to push that about.

One evening, after the kids had gone and it was getting dark, he heard a noise from outside his tank. The cat had come to torment him again.

McQueen was the school cat. An old Scottish ginger tom, that paraded around the school like he owned it, and Peter was scared of him, which was just as well because McQueen's intentions were never going to be friendly. He would sit on top of the tank and take swings at Peter through the hole, hoping to hook him out and eat him.

He'd first met McQueen one evening when the children had gone, and the school was empty and quiet. He had squeezed out of a hole between the wooden floorboards and the skirting on the back wall and wandered around the classroom looking for food. This particular day, one of the children had spilled a bag of potato crisps onto the floor and they had been trampled everywhere as the children had left.

Peter had been so busy hoovering up all these lovely scraps, he hadn't noticed the cat creep into the classroom.

'Weel, hellooo, and what d'we 'ave 'ere noo?'

Startled, Peter jumped as a huge set of claws swiped beneath him. He ran as fast as he could back towards his hole, but when he reached it, he realised he eaten too much and couldn't get through, so he dived off to his right, narrowly avoiding the claws that combed his back.

Peter leapt for a chair that hadn't been tucked under a desk. He missed and ended up going beneath it, which was fortunate because the cat had anticipated his move and was already on the chair, waiting.

On landing back on the floor, Peter scooted towards a set of low-level shelves with papers on and took a jump for a shelf as the claws swung to one side of him.

As he reached the shelf, he immediately took off again for the next one and again for the one after that. He was now at window level, and he leapt again for another shelf as the cat jumped up, almost catching him.

Suddenly, he fell. He had landed in a dusty aquarium, through the hole in the top and now a large blue eye surrounded by ginger fur looked down on him.

'Yummmmy,' said the cat, licking his lips, 'Dinna is served.'

Peter shook with fear and cowered in a corner. The cat swung his paws repeatedly but couldn't quite reach him. He got off the lid and peered at him through the glass at the side, frustration etched all over his face. His claws scratched at the glass but made no impression, and eventually, after many, many minutes the cat wandered off. Peter was terrified. He didn't know where he was, and he couldn't get out.

And that was how he was found in the morning when one of the children noticed this little bundle of brown fur curled up and shaking in the corner of the tank.

The kids all crowded around, scaring Peter all over again, and pleaded with their teacher to be able to keep him and look after him.

The teacher said, that on the condition they kept him clean, fed, and watered, they could keep him.

Over the weeks, he learned that the children weren't going to hurt him, and he allowed them to handle him. He actually enjoyed the attention and started to relax in their company.

He loved the kids that looked after him. That cleaned his home, fed him, and filled up his water bottle. He really liked the ones that picked him up and put him in and out of the bird cage.

He disliked, however, being cooped up at the weekend, where he had no-one for company and nobody to talk to, other than McQueen, of course. Not that McQueen had a lot of conversation. His threats of death and violence kept Peter on his toes, and he knew if one of McQueen's swings ever caught him, he would be in serious trouble.

He was always nervous when the cat came around.

McQueen

It was several weeks later he was able to sneak out and revisit classroom 6. He sat on top of the tank, repeatedly swinging his claws, but could not reach his prey. Eventually, he realised he would have to find a different way to get it.

'Dinna' keep movin' aboot ya lil' monster, I'm only gonna eat ya.' McQueen had said to him, when he had sat on top of the cage trying desperately to hook the mouse out.

But, frustrated, he went home to formulate another way of catching him.

The horrible children had taken the rodent as a pet. He'd been given food and water and now they had put a wheel in the tank for the mouse to play on.

McQueen spent time hiding and watching from outside the classroom to see what the mouse did with his evenings.

His reconnaissance had revealed that the mouse would sneak out at night and McQueen knew he would have another chance to catch it soon. How he wanted that mouse.

Peter Mouse

One evening when McQueen was nowhere in sight, Peter pushed his pencil into the bottom of the wheel. He had come up with a plan to get out and tonight was the night he was going to do it.

The pencil jammed the wheel and stopped it turning, and Peter climbed slowly and carefully up the outside of the wheel until he reached the top. The hole in the lid was just above him but as he went to jump, the wheel moved the other way and he missed the hole, hitting the underside of the lid and falling back to the shavings on the floor.

Peter was angry with himself. He had not expected the wheel to roll backwards. He went to the pencil and this time he pushed it through the bars of the wheel until it stuck out on both sides. This should stop the wheel revolving in either direction, he hoped.

He climbed the wheel again and this time, when he jumped, he went up, straight through the hole and landed safely on his feet, on top of the lid.

He stopped and looked around. He couldn't see or hear the cat, so cautiously he skipped down the shelves to the classroom floor.

He made his way over to where his hole in the skirting was, but Peter was a lot bigger now and he couldn't get through.

He wasn't sure what to do next. He thought he would be able to escape to the outside world through that hole and he hadn't considered anything else.

McQueen

This evening he had watched the children leave at the end of their day. He snuck in and lay on a chair that wasn't tucked under its' desk. The room grew quiet, and the light began to fade, and he watched the mouse leave the aquarium, climb down to the floor and head towards where he was hiding. The ambush was set.

He waited until the mouse was within reach then leapt down and swung his paw, catching the mouse on its' body and knocking it a metre away. The mouse went skidding across the floor and the cat set off to finish it.

Although he was winded, the mouse jumped onto a chair that was tucked under a desk and McQueen leapt right behind it, realising too late that there wasn't enough room for him to get up.

He collided with the underside of the desk and landed back on the floor with a grunt. He ignored the pain in his head and raced after the little rodent. He had completely lost his temper.

He watched the mouse scamper up the shelves and dive back into the aquarium, to land safely among the shavings.

McQueen was just a second behind him. He sat and swung his claws again and again, his tail swishing furiously.

He swung at the wheel but only hurt a claw when it freewheeled around and caught him unexpectedly. Outraged, he clouted the wheel and completely knocked it over, hoping it might pierce the mouse and mean his evening wouldn't be wasted.

'Ya' wee monster, I'm gonna get ya', an' when I do, ya' gonna beg me ta' eat ya'.

With more choice words said, he left. The evening ending as many had done before. He slunk away, miaowing loudly, barely in control of himself.

Peter Mouse

Peter laid on his shavings in a corner, his heartrate slowly recovering, and smiled up at his adversary. He poked out his tongue at the cat, but secretly, he knew he had been lucky.

He could hear the cat miaowing loudly all the way down the corridor and he let out a long sigh. That certainly had been close. Next time he'd have to stay alert, and he'll have to find another way out.

The following morning when the children saw the wheel on its' side, they decided that Peter must have somehow knocked it over in the night, so they put him in the birdcage while the teacher glued the wheel to the floor of the tank.

When he was returned, later that afternoon, he realised he would still be able to get out and the fact that the wheel wouldn't fall over gave him more confidence.

Peter had another plan on how to get away. He put his ping-pong ball on the floor of his tank and practised jumping on the nearest edge of it to make the ball skid away from him.

He was doing this often enough to hit the wheel with it regularly, but the sound it made attracted the attention of McQueen. He sat on the tank and peered at him through the hole in the lid.

'Are ya' no' comin' oot ta' play?' the cat said, sarcastically, 'I'm gonna eat ya' anyway, it might as well be tonight.'

Peter ignored him and went into his wheel. He started running as fast as he could. The cat withdrew the claw he'd had near the wheel and put an eye to the hole.

At full speed, Peter jumped out of the wheel, leaving it spinning and ran back to where his ball sat. He jumped on the side of the ball as hard as he could, and it went flying into the wheel. And, because it was spinning, the ball was thrown off at tremendous speed.

It hit McQueen smack in his eye, and he yelped so loud Peter thought his head had fallen off.

Peter retired to a corner as the cat hissed and miaowed like crazy. He jumped up and down on the tank lid in his anger, but his eye was watering so much he couldn't see, and the noise was enough to make the girl come in to find out what was going on.

McQueen

He had been jumping up and down on the lid of the tank in his fury, spitting and hissing like never before when hands lifted him up and away from the tank and he looked up to see the girl telling him off, but in his rage, he couldn't understand what she was saying. Nor did he care. He wanted that mouse, and he wanted it dead.

The next day, after school had finished, he put another plan into action. He climbed up onto the lockers outside classroom 6 and laid in wait. He figured the mouse would show sooner or later. He needed to be patient.

Sure enough, just as it started to get dark, the mouse popped its' head around the door.

He wanted to jump on it there and then but held himself back.

The mouse then made a mistake. It climbed onto the very locker McQueen was hiding on. As it looked over the top it was nose to nose with the cat.

Bang came down the ginger paw, almost catching its' tail as it turned to run. Down leapt McQueen, through the classroom door, right behind the little rodent it hated with a vengeance.

Just as he was about to swat it, the mouse changed direction. McQueen skidded and turned. He saw it race up the leg of the teachers' desk, so he leapt up the other side to cut it off.

Peter Mouse

Earlier that evening, Peter had jumped up onto the lid of his tank. This time he had his ping-pong ball in his mouth. Where it was dented, he had bitten into it, and it allowed him to carry it in his mouth.

He carefully looked around to make sure he wasn't going to be pounced on, and satisfied he was alone, he hopped down to the floor and across to the teachers' desk, where he climbed up and put the ball near the edge. Then he sat back behind the pencil sharpener and waited for the light to go.

As it got dark, he climbed down and walked carefully towards the open door. He knew the cat was around, but he didn't know where.

He stopped at the door and peered quickly around the corner into the corridor. He saw nothing but his awareness was high. Peter climbed easily up the nearest set of lockers and peered over the top. Straight into a swollen blue eye and a large ginger face.

'Oops,' he said to himself jumping clear. He landed lightly, on the floor and bolted back towards his tank. The ginger cat was clawing at his tail as they went through the classroom door and getting closer every second.

Suddenly Peter veered off to his right, scooted up the teachers desk and waited behind his ball. A second later the ginger face appeared above desk, as Peter knew he would.

Peter jumped on his ball. It flew straight and true and hit the cat in his one remaining good eye.

The cat screamed and fell to the floor. He shot out of the classroom door so fast he crashed into the lockers opposite. He screamed again and ran off towards the door that led to his quarters.

McQueen

McQueen didn't remember much of what had happened. He knew he'd crashed into some lockers because his head hurt, but he couldn't see so he wasn't sure.

When the girl saw him in the morning she screamed. That brought her father running and he put the cat in a box and off they went to the vet.

McQueen hated the vet with as much venom as that mouse. He hissed and spat and refused to allow the vet to work on him.

Finally, having run out of patience, the vet managed to inject the cat with a tranquiliser, which gave him time for an inspection.

On his return home McQueen was closely watched and with a cone over his head to prevent him scratching his eyes, he was kept indoors. His eyes were bruised and sore but would recover with no damage. This did not improve his temper at all.

It was over a week before McQueen managed to creep into classroom 6 again. He pretended nothing was wrong, but he was seething inside. He jumped onto the tank lid and exchanged a few words, well, threats actually

Peter Mouse

Peter watched as McQueen sauntered up towards his tank and sat on the lid.

'How's the eyes?' he asked the cat as it fished around with a claw.

'Ya' wee monster, ya'll regret dealin' wi' me. Ya'll wish ya'd stayed in ya' lil' hole. I'll getcha', mark me words, I'll getcha,' was all the cat said, as it wandered off and out of sight.

The next morning, the cat came in early. He didn't usually appear until the afternoon, but again he was in a foul mood.

He had watched the cleaners do their work and leave. He wandered in and sat on the shelf, to one side of the tank and eyed the mouse aggressively.

He put his nose under the lid and started pushing up. The lid moved. He pushed a bit harder, and the lid lifted more.

Encouraged by this, McQueen pushed again, this time standing on his back legs. The lid lifted and when the cat pushed harder, the lid moved further.

The lid popped up and sat on the lip of the tank. Slowly, the cat pushed the lid further and further across, exposing the interior, first by a little, then by a lot. He now had his head inside the tank.

Peter was terrified. He was so scared, he couldn't move. He couldn't even take his eyes off the cat when its' head appeared inside.

McQueen then lifted a paw and stretched it in and put it down, pushing with his shoulders to move the lid further away. His other front leg followed straight away. All the time his eyes were locked onto Peter's.

McQueen broke eye contact to lift a rear leg in and Peter suddenly realised how much trouble he was in. He dived for the bottom of the wheel to try and hide, but the cat was now inside the tank.

He crept around the wheel and struck at Peter with a sharp claw. Peter felt it strike home and no matter how hard he huddled under the wheel, he couldn't keep out of McQueen's reach. He would get him. He knew he had nowhere left to go and started shaking with fear.

Then a noise from the corridor distracted the cat. It grew louder and louder and as the children came charging into the classroom, ready for register and lessons, a couple of the girls screamed.

They had seen McQueen in the tank, and they ran to him. A girl grabbed him and lifted him out quickly. She heavily dropped him to the floor, and he slunk off and away.

The whole class gathered around as best they could, trying to see what had happened and the teacher was made aware of what had been seen.

One of the boys gently lifted Peter out from where he had been cowering under the wheel, and carefully looked him over for body damage.

There was blood on his back and neck, but these were just scratches. Peter was then washed and disinfected.

For the next ten minutes Peter continued to shake, but slowly calmed down enough for a boy to put him into his blazer top pocket, with his head out so he could see, and Peter fell into a short fitful sleep.

The teacher adjusted the lid of the tank so it fitted better and couldn't be lifted off in that way again.

Peter slowly became less nervous as the day wore on and it was decided that the boy whose pocket Peter had slept in would take him home for a few days as there were no other pets at his house,

The tank came with them, and the boys' mother was astonished to see what he had brought home. Until that was, she heard the story of what McQueen had done.

For the rest of that week Peter stayed with the boys' family and over the weekend he accompanied the boy in his jacket top pocket, wherever he went.

Peter recovered from his ordeal quickly and both he and the tank returned to school the following week. Again, at the weekend, the boy took him out in his pocket and looked after him. Peter loved every minute of it. This was what he had wanted all the time.

At school, Peter was in his tank when McQueen sauntered in. He sat at the side of his tank and tried to nose the lid up. It didn't move. He tried scratching at the glass. Peter had started shaking with fear again.

He knew then that he would have to leave if he was ever to get over what had happened.

He made a plan and decided to carry it out that day. The boy lifted him into his pocket to go out at lunchtime as usual, and he waited until he was outside in the school grounds. There, he jumped out of the boys' pocket to the ground and scampered away into the undergrowth.

Several of the children tried to recapture him but he was too quick and nimble.

He disappeared into the shrubland and headed for the safety of the hedgerow by the path.

He found a little burrow beneath a bush and settled there until everyone had gone home.

When it was dark, he ventured out to investigate his surroundings. He felt better than he had for a while. There were some fallen apples on the ground, and he ate them hungrily.

He heard a snuffling noise behind him, and a hedgehog came into sight. He watched it pull up a worm and slurp it down in one gulp.

They spoke and the hedgehog told Peter where he could find food and water. He slept in the burrow at night and felt safe knowing that the cat was nowhere around.

Morning came, and with it a lot of foot traffic nearby, as the children made their way to school. Peter watched from under a bush. He missed his class.

After several weeks of surviving in the burrow, Peter was thinking of going back, when another little mouse appeared. She was smaller than him and very frightened.

She said her name was Sukie and she had escaped from a pet shop. She was tired of being cooped up all day and night with nothing to do.

He welcomed her in and told her to stay for as long as she wanted. He was grateful for the company and to be honest, for someone to talk to.

Peter told her the story of the cat and they laughed at how he bashed both of its' eyes and Sukie talked of the monotony at the pet shop where no-one bothered to clean the cage and frequently forgot to feed and water her, and that she didn't ever want to return. Peter told her about the boy and his family and suggested that if he went back to classroom 6, perhaps she would like to accompany him.

Sukie agreed. She'd never lived anywhere but the pet shop and it all sounded rather good.

Peter waited until school was finishing and hid beside a bush, waiting for the boy to appear. But as he saw him, he heard a cry behind him.

McQueen

McQueen had taken to patrolling the grounds, hoping for an unsuspecting bird to come his way.

For the last few weeks, he had been barred from entering the classrooms. Then one lunchtime, someone had left a door open, and he snuck in only to find the tank empty.

He hoped he had scared the mouse to death and smiled to himself as he did so.

It was as he was patrolling the school grounds near the path, one afternoon, he picked up a familiar scent.

Silently, he followed it. Creeping on his stomach so as not to be seen, he saw a mouse in a hollow. It wasn't the mouse he wanted, but he figured, one mouse is as good as another.

He pounced. He landed on the tail and picked the mouse up in his teeth. Then he noticed his enemy.

Peter Mouse

Peter turned. Standing there, with the little mouse in its' mouth, was McQueen.

He spat her out.

'Weel halloo agin, Peter Mouse. I think ya' 'n me got some lil' business ta' finish.'

Peter's stomach turned and he felt his heart rate rising. There was going to be a fight. He saw Sukie try to move away, but McQueen had his foot on her tail. She was so scared she was shaking.

'No so fast lil' 'un, I'll be 'aving ya' fer dinna too,' he said without taking his eyes off Peter, 'after I've 'ad that 'un.'

Peter went into action and leapt upwards towards the cats' right ear. McQueen's right foot was holding Sukie down so it couldn't stop the attack.

Peter bit the ear as he landed, then took off again straight away, landing on the cats' tail so he bit that too. The cat yelled and jumped up, surprised by the attack, and Sukie dived for cover under a bush.

McQueen turned and swung a claw at Peter but missed. However, Peter was still in range and was caught by the next swing. It knocked him onto the path where several children were walking home. He landed well and turned to see his attacker jumping at him. Peter quickly ran forward, but the cat, landing behind him, turned and swung another blow, and this caught Peter on the neck.

He ended up on the grass verge beside the road and slowly picked himself up. He was covered in blood.

McQueen was now strutting slowly towards him. The fight was almost over. He could picture eating Peter Mouse for dinner and the little one for afters.

He reached Peter, who still stood and faced him, and while he admired the bravery of one so small, he considered him stupid for not running away.

Now it was time to eat. McQueen stuck out his paw to hold him down, but Peter had moved. He had taken a couple of steps backwards and was now on the road kerbstone itself. The cat lowered its' head and approached again.

This time Peter sprang forward and bit the cats' nose. McQueen jumped and stuck a heavy paw on Peter as it landed, holding him down.

Suddenly, and from nowhere, another mouse landed on the cats' tail and bit as hard as it could. McQueen yelped, jumped, and sprang forward to escape the attacker. Straight into the road and straight into the path of an oncoming vehicle. The sound seemed to kill time, and everything happened in slow motion.

The car skidded to a halt, but the cat continued to fly several metres down the road. Sukie, who had bitten the cats' tail, ran over to see if Peter was still alive. He was, but barely.

Some of the children who had witnessed the fight were crying. One of the boys had come over to see if there was anything he could do. It was the boy whose pocket

Peter had lived in for a while. He went to pick Peter up, but Sukie stood in front of him and bared her teeth.

Exhausted, Peter could hardly lift his head, but he said quietly, 'Sukie, it's alright. This is the boy I told you about. He's ok.'

Sukie backed off, but as the boy lifted Peter up, she jumped onto his hands and laid down beside her man. She wasn't letting anyone get between them ever again.

A couple of teachers had come over to see what the commotion was about, and were consoling the car driver, while the school caretaker had to pick up what was left of McQueen.

Peter and Sukie were carried to the boys' house where his mother dealt with

Peter's wounds and cleaned them as well as she could.

It was touch and go for a couple of days, but Peter was a strong mouse and as he recovered, Sukie helped look after him as well.

Several weeks later, the boy took Peter and Sukie back to school where they were celebrated and cheered as they returned to the tank. The whole class were amazed at how well he had recovered.

A week later, they were even more amazed to find half a dozen new-born youngsters in the tank with them. Bald, blind, and pink, these little ones were the talk of the school and Peter was the proudest father ever.

One day, he would tell them about the ginger cat and how their mother had saved his life. But not today. Today, he had a family to look after and lots of human friends to play with.

Printed in Great Britain
by Amazon